The Legend

The Mystery of Herobrine, Book Three - Herobrine versus the World (The Unofficial Minecraft Adventure Story)

Mark Mulle

PUBLISHED BY:
Mark Mulle
Copyright © 2014

Disclaimer
This is a work of fiction. Names, characters, businesses, places, events and incidents are either the products of the author's imagination or used in fictitious manny. Any resemblance to actual persons, living or dead, or actual events is purely coincidental.

Author's Note: This short story is for your reading pleasure. The characters in this "Minecraft Adventure Series" such as Steve, Endermen or Herobrine...etc are based on the Minecraft Game coming from Minecraft ®/TM & © 2009-2013 Mojang / Notch

I was downright frightened by the whole scene, a giant army being mass-produced in the underground. What was the point of all this? Was there going to be an invasion of some sorts?

But before I could think anything of it, the mine cart rushed away into yet another room, a much smaller one where I saw something even more disturbing. If the previous room looked pretty much like your average underground cave, this one looked nothing like it. All the walls were made out of red bricks, similar to the ones that were inside Micah's stronghold, nether bricks, as they called them, and small trenches filled with lava and burning pits of fire were everywhere I looked. The pathway, on which the railroad was a few feet above from the ground and ahead of it, at the very end, was a small tower in the middle of a shimmering purple sea. Everywhere I looked I started seeing these sinister monsters that looked like a cross between a human zombie and a pig. The cart quickly drew their attention and all of them suddenly turned around and started staring at it. I quickly reached the end of the tracks and got out of the mine cart. I was now inside of the tower. There were no torches inside the tower, which meant that it was pretty dark, apart from the light provided by the lava and by the fire pits. I drew my sword and slowly walked up the stairs. The tower seemed empty. I reached the top and found a small wooden chest. I looked inside it and found a diamond sword, some torches, some cooked pork chops and an emerald. I emptied the chest of all of its contents and as

I turned around to take a good look at my surroundings I saw that I wasn't alone. A tall, black skeleton, one like I had never seen before was standing right in front of me.

The black skeleton started grunting. I froze in terror in front of it. Then, after a couple of seconds of complete and utter silence he said:

"He…is….not…here. Why…are…you…here?"

I struggled to think of something to say, but nothing came out. The skeleton then said:

"Why…are…you…here?"

"I'm the new guy," I managed to mumble. "Micah sent me over to check on you guys, to make sure that everyone is doing their jobs."

"Who…are…you?" The big black skeleton asked me in his deep growly voice.

"I'm…"

But the skeleton didn't wait for an answer. Instead he growled loudly, so loud, in fact, that all of the room seemed to echo along with him.

It was then that out of the blue, I jumped on top of the chest, looked over the railing and took a leap of faith down into the shimmering lake. I don't know why I did it, but it was a good thing that I did, because just at that moment the skeleton slashed at me with his giant black sword. He nearly hit me, but by the time he pulled back to take another swing I was halfway down to the shimmering purple lake.

And then I hit the purple waves. My fall abruptly stopped once I hit the surface of the lake and my vision started shaking. It all went dark and when I could finally see what was going on, I was in a place that I had never seen before, ever.

The ground was reddish and it made a sandy noise, a sort of "swoosh" when I made each step. I walked cautiously, looking in every direction. Everything was either red or dark red. Fires were wherever I looked. This had to be the Netherland. Jerry was right: it was the scariest place in Minecraft. I walked for about five minutes until I saw a change in scenery. I saw this tower that was made out of dark blocks, and at the top of the tower I saw something that look like a portal. The portal was made out of some sort of black bricks that formed a ring around a purple shimmering veil, similar to the one through which I fell t. I knew that in order to get back to the surface world, I had to go through that portal.

And so, I made my way up to the tower.

The coast looked clear but as I made my way to the tower I could see that I was walking on top of a cliff and that to my right was a giant lake of lava and that to my right there was a sort of irregularly-shaped hill. On the hill there were a lot of those zombie pigmen that I saw earlier. They seemed pretty passive to me. The pigmen wielded a sword and seemed pretty tough, but at the same time, they weren't aggressive at all. They just stood there and looked at me, which was more than good. I couldn't see myself winning a battle with that many of them, anyways.

I think I must have had to walk ten more feet in order to reach the tower, when I heard this awful screech that sounded like someone was crying out in pain. The shout came from my right, from down where the lava was. I turned right and as I approached the edge of the cliff I could see this giant, cloudlike shape rise from down below. When the creature rose up above the side of the cliff, up into the air above me it started looking more like a giant, cube-shaped ghost more than anything. It had a sad face on its front part and it kept screaming at me. Then, the ghostly figure started firing fireballs at me. The first one caught me off my guard and hit me directly in the chest. It was a good thing that I was wearing my armor or else I think that I would have been blown to dust. But the fireball did hurt me. It took a sizeable portion off my health bar and it sent me flying back a couple of feet. The second fireball I managed to dodge. I then quickly ran inside the tower, where some sort of burning monster, one that also threw fireballs at me, greeted me. This one was made out of a bunch of yellow rods that danced around in a cloud of pitch-black smoke, with a small yellow head that had two black eyes on the front of it. I managed to steer clear of its fireballs and landed a whole lot of blows with my meager iron sword before the monster eventually perished, leaving behind something called a blaze rod, an item with which I had virtually no idea how to use.

After dispatching of this blaze monster, I ran as fast as I could to the top of the tower. But when I reached the tower, I saw that the large ghost monster, or ghast, as I later found out it was called, was waiting for me. Luckily I was already on my guard and managed to dodge the incoming fireballs that it threw at me. I figured that I could have taken down this monster if I would have had a bow and a hefty amount of arrows with me, but it was no time to think about that too much. I took a mental note anyway that the next time that I was going to travel to the Nether I had to bring with me a bow and a whole lot of arrows.

I dodged about four or five fireballs and then quickly jumped through the portal. The lights went out yet again, leaving me in complete and utter darkness for a few seconds. When I woke up, I found myself standing on top of a mountain, looking down and seeing Micah's village.

It was nighttime, but I wasn't going to just build myself a shelter and spend the night hiding in it. I decided I was going to climb down from the mountain and make my way back to my hideout, under the cover of the night. I started running down the side of the mountain when I saw a beam of purple light going up from somewhere on the ground and piercing the sky. It was like nothing that I had ever seen before. It was majestic and terrifying at the same time, as I knew that it had something to do with what was probably a grand plot that belonged either to Micah or to Herobrine, or worse, to both of them.

I then started making my way towards the source of the beam of light that turned out to be on the right side of the mountain, somewhere halfway from the top to the foot of the mountain. I ran as fast as I could in order to find the source.

I got closer and closer and as I passed a final ridge I could see that the beam of light was coming from what looked like a camp that was concentrated around a thin tall tower that had a wide platform on its top. When I got even closer to the whole site, the camp turned out to be some sort of temple. From where I stood, I could see a bunch of people standing on the wide platform atop the tower. I moved from cover to cover, managing to remain out of sight, behind whatever rocks I could find. When I got close enough I started to make out who the people on the platform were. One of them had a full set of diamond armor on him, another had a black helmet on and the others wore matching iron armors. It was clear that they were Micah, Zeke and their henchmen. That meant that the village was all but empty, apart from my friend Jerry who was probably left behind to guard the place.

That moment I knew that it was my chance to go there and let him in on what I had found out. But as I turned around, I saw movement on the side of the mountain from where I came. I remained hidden behind my cover. I peeked over the cover and took a quick glance. It was shaped like a human. Maybe it was a zombie, or maybe it was another player. Either way, I was going to sit tight and wait for it to come to me, that way I could easily ambush it and hightail it out of there in order to warn my friend Jerry. The monster came closer and closer, as I could easily hear its steps louder and louder. When I thought it was the right moment, I jumped out swinging my sword left and right. But I didn't get to land any blows because it turned out my monster, wasn't really a monster after all. It was my friend Jerry.

"What are you doing here, Jerry? Seriously, I could have clobbered you to death," I told him.

"I didn't know you were going to be here, Mike. Plus, you couldn't clobber me to death with that dull blade of yours. I followed Micah and the guys. They've never left the camp on "official business" during the night, so naturally I had to check it out and see what was up, you know. I saw them going through here and then I saw that giant beam of light springing up towards the sky. I figured that something nasty was happening. What are you doing here?"

"Long story. It turns out that Micah or Herobrine, or both of them are connecting this world with the Nether. They're bringing all sorts of creatures through the portals and they are gathering a giant army of mobs in underground caves. I don't know exactly what it is that they are trying to accomplish but I don't think that it's anything nice. I managed to pass through the Nether and back here. Somehow I ended up coming back from the Nether right here on this mountain."

"Wow. Look at what an adventurer you have become, Mike. Nice. That reminds me, I wanted to give you something. You know those wooden chests that you found down in the cellar?"

"Yeah sure. They were filled with diamonds and TNT and all sorts of stuff."

"Yeah well, I took some stuff out of a smaller one that wasn't in the back of the bigger ones. And I thought that I should put it to good use, so here!"

Jerry opened his inventory and out of it he threw a diamond breastplate, a diamond set of grieves, a diamond set of boots and a diamond sword. He also threw some dynamite blocks onto the ground, as well.

"After all, an adventurer needs the best equipment, doesn't he?"

"Wow, Jerry. Thanks a lot! This is amazing."

"Yeah, sure. My pleasure. Look, in order to use the TNT, you just put it down wherever you want to blow stuff up and then set fire to it with your flint and steel. Oh and get as far away as possible, especially when you place more than one block somewhere."

"I'll be sure to remember that, Jerry. But what are we going to do now?"

Jerry took a long look at the tower that emitted the tall purple beam of light. After that he turned to me and said.

"Look, whatever they're doing there, it doesn't look good. Their trips to secret locations have been increasing these past weeks and I'm afraid whatever their final goal might be, they are getting pretty close to accomplishing it."

"So what are we going to do about it? Surely we have to do something," I said to him.

"Let's start by getting a closer look at whatever they have built there."

It seemed like a good enough starting point for me. And so, together we got closer and closer to the temple where Micah and his acolytes were doing their dark deeds.

When we reached the bottom of the temple, we saw that it had no way in. There were no doors, no windows, not a single tunnel or any other point of entry…that is, except for a Nether portal that was on one side of the base of the building.

Jerry and I walked up to the portal and I jumped in first.

When we passed through to the Nether we were inside a dark room. Jerry started setting torches around us so that we could better see our surroundings. The room was pretty big, except for the fact that the ceiling was only two blocks high, and our heads almost grazed it while we walked around. We started walking to the end of the room and climbed up a ladder to the next level. The next level turned out to be full of pigmen. These guys were literally everywhere.

"Whatever you do, don't hit them. They may hit you, but never hit them back," said Jerry.

"Don't worry I won't," I assured him. I wasn't the noob I used to be. By that point I had seen a lot of stuff, stuff that most Minecraft players don't even dream about.

We gradually made our way through the sea of pigmen that flooded the second level of the building that we were inside of until we reached the ladder that went up to the third floor.

The third floor was flooded with lava, which in a way was good because the molten lava lit up the place so we could see what was ahead of us. The bad part was that the way to the ladder that led to the next level of the building was way back over to the other side of the room. Also, the path to reach it was made out of scattered blocks that were apart from each other at irregular distances. Basically we either had to leap from block to block or we had to build a path to the ladder ourselves. Seeing that we weren't actually pressured to hurry, we decided that we would build our own path and connect the blocks to each other in order to reach the ladder. Jerry took the initiative and started laying down blocks to build the walkway. It took some time but we eventually managed to reach the ladder and climb up to the next level.

This level looked pretty empty. But out of the darkness three dark skeletons appeared.

"Withers! Watch out!" said Jerry.

I equipped my new and shiny diamond sword and started attacking the skeleton that was the nearest to us. While I was doing that, Jerry equipped his bow and arrows and started firing at the other two, knocking them back to make sure that I wouldn't get overwhelmed. I quickly destroyed the first Wither Skeleton and when I got next to the next one I heard a strange clicking sound from underneath my feet. It was then that holes opened up on each wall and a whole load of strange, dark red and black cube-like monsters started pouring into the room. The withers didn't seem to be bothered at all by the magma cubes and continued to slash their giant black swords at us. I managed to dispatch of the second wither much easier than I did the first one, mostly because Jerry had weakened it with his arrows. But there was no time to destroy the third one, because in a matter of seconds we were overrun by those darned magma cubes. I managed to land a couple of blows to the wither, just enough to provide Jerry with some cover so that he could move closer to the ladder. Then, once I made sure Jerry was safe past the wither I ran right behind him, trying to avoid touching or getting touched by any of those magma cubes. Along the way I bashed some of the magma cubes, only to find out that once you destroy them, they turn into smaller ones. That being said, fighting them would have turned out to be a pointless battle that would have not only slowed us down but it would have also put a strain on us and our resources.

We quickly climbed up the ladder and saw that we were on top of the building. But not only did we realize that there were no more levels to go, we also realized that we were sitting on top of the base of what looked like an exact replica of the temple from the Overworld. We then saw the thin tower that had the wide platform on top of it and we also saw that on top of the tower there was a similar beam of light to the one from the Overworld, but this one pierced the stone ceiling that was in place of the normal sky down here in the Nether.

As we looked for the way up to the platform we saw a long ladder that went from the bottom of the thin tower all the way up to the top where the platform was.

We quickly ran up to the ladder and climbed it all the way to the top, reaching the platform. Upon reaching the platform we finally saw what was the source of the beam – a strange pyramid-shaped contraption made out of gold blocks, diamond blocks, obsidian and some other things that I could not recognize. On top of the pyramid there was a small fire, and from that fire came out a beam of light that gradually widened until it became so massive that you could see it from far, far away.

What we also saw on that platform was a Nether portal.

Before going through the portal, Jerry stopped and said:

"Look, Mike, be extra careful. These guys are pretty good, and they outnumber us three-to-one. Plus, we don't know if these guys have Herobrine with them. Just be careful. Keep your distance from Micah and Zeke, because they're pretty good with the sword. And if you go against the archers, use the same tactic that you use for skeletons. Just be careful, and I'm sure that we can get through this just fine."

"I'll be careful, Jerry. You be careful, too!"

"Will do. Let's get them!"

And with that we walked through the Nether portal.

When we came out of the portal and into the Overworld, we were standing on the temple's platform right on the opposite sides from Micah and his goons.

Jerry and I didn't wait for them to say hello and each of us attacked them from one side, going around the pyramid on the center of the platform. I attacked the four archers and Jerry went for Zeke and Micah.

The archers fired arrow after arrow at me. I managed to dodge the first four but got hit by the next two arrows. The impact knocked me back a foot or two, but I kept my composure and started swinging my sword at the nearest archer. He tried to hit me with his arrows but I caught him with a good combination of hits and the last one sent him falling over the platform. But the other three took this opportunity to riddle me with arrows as they scattered around the platform to become more difficult targets. If I had been wearing a set of armor made out of iron I would have been running for my life by that point, but luckily I had a diamond set of armor on me, which meant I could take more hits.

I ran towards the nearest archer and managed to use my diamond sword to shove him off the platform and send him flying into the air and then falling quickly to the ground.

On the other side of the platform, Micah had apparently vanished and Zeke kept battling with Jerry. Both of them were wearing iron armors and wielding iron swords. I didn't quite get why Micah was the only one who wore a diamond set of armor. I mean, I knew that the others could have diamond tools or swords and I had seen Jerry wielding a diamond axe before. But maybe diamonds were used for other purposes...such as helping to build these mysterious contraptions and they were not to be wasted on a lot of other things.

My little moment of introspection proved to be near deadly for me, as I almost didn't manage to keep myself from falling after being knocked back by an arrow that was fired by one of the archers. Luckily, I managed to avoid being knocked off the ledge by jumping almost instantly as I saw the arrow coming. That way I controlled myself while in midair so that I could land back safely onto the platform. I then ran towards the archer and hit him with my sword repeatedly. And with each hit he got knocked back further and further until he had nowhere else to go. His back was to the pyramid that fired the light beam. And with the last hit, he got knocked off directly into the purple ray. He tried to get out of it, but it was too late. He got practically disintegrated by the beam.

The remaining archer, seeing that his three friends didn't have any luck against me, tried to make a run through the portal in order to escape through the nether. But that proved to be a bad idea, because in his mix of haste and fear, he forgot to stop and wait to be teleported on through to the other side. Instead of doing that, he kept running and because he didn't stop at the right time, he went right through the thin purple veil and fell off the platform. Poor fool.

After the archers were gone, I opened my inventory and grabbed a quick bite to eat in order to regain my health before setting out to help Jerry battle Zeke. When my health bar was back up again, I ran up to where Zeke was fighting Jerry and I started wailing on Zeke with my sword. Seeing that he was clearly no match for the both of us, Zeke threw a glass bottle at us that had a poisonous liquid inside it. The bottle hit Jerry and only he took the damage from the poison. Zeke then tried to make a charge at me, but his blade, was no match for my armor. I managed to withstand three of his blows, and launched my own terrible attack, swinging my diamond sword left and right, pushing him to the edge of the platform. At that point Zeke said:

"Okay. It's over, you win!"

Jerry and I looked over at each other. Then Jerry said:

"Okay Zeke, just put down your sword and we can talk about this"

Zeke stood there in silent for a second or two then he started laughing.

"Ha! Do you really think that I would surrender to a couple of noobs like you two? Not a chance. No way in Nether am I going to surrender. I just don't want to give you two "heroes" a chance to defeat me like this. I'd rather respawn and lose my gear than be defeated by a couple of slime cubes like you. You'll see, once the boss succeeds in his deal with Herobrine, we'll be kings over this world. See ya!"

And with that he jumped. Jerry and I looked down and saw Zeke turn into a small cloud of dust and leave behind a lot of items that hovered above the ground.

I turned to Jerry:

"What now? He'll probably just respawn back at the village. As a matter of fact, they will all spawn back at the village and eventually come and get us."

Jerry laughed and said:

"Well, yeah. They will respawn, Mike, but they will have quite a nice surprise when they do and I'm afraid that they will have to respawn once more, but not in the village."

I didn't quite understand what Jerry meant by that the first time, but once he explained it to me, I laughed even harder than he did. It went a little something like this:

Jerry suspected the fact that something big was about to happen that night and if it did, that would have meant that he would have needed to leave the camp, find me so that we could try and defeat those guys. And to make our jobs easier, he rigged their village with explosive. And so when they did finally come back to the village, or just respawned near their beds, the whole thing would blow up sky high. With the beds being destroyed, the respawn point would reset to its original location, and who knows how far that meant. In any case that gave us a pretty good advantage over them. With his team scattered and with his precious village in ruins, Micah would be easier to defeat. And that was exactly what we were going to do. But first we had to find him.

After we had our good laugh and recovered our forces after the battle, I turned to Jerry.

"So where do you think Micah went, Jerry?"

"That guy is full of tricks. He jumped off the platform as soon as I got close to him."

"So does that mean that he also went up in smoke along with the rest of the gang?"

"Not really. He didn't need to respawn. He jumped off the platform and he had an ender pearl with him. He threw the ender pearl away and teleported himself onto the mountain side."

"Did you rig the whole village with explosives?"

"No, I didn't have enough time; else I would have risked losing them. I planted as much as I could and rigged it as fast as I could. But if he reached the village he might have…Do you think that he's there, Mike?"

"He might be, since the tunnel that he had in his cellar led to what looked like a pretty big base or something. I think that we should check it out."

And so we ran as fast as we could in order to reach the village. When we reached it, we both saw the full extent of the damage from Jerry's little explosive experiment only when we got through the stone passage. Most of the houses were in ruins. All the villagers were huddled up inside a small shack in the corner of the yard. All of the animals had invaded the yard, because a portion of the fence that used to keep them inside their pens was blown away. The houses that belonged to the players had been turned to rubble. But the stone stronghold remained untouched. The doors were wide open, though.

"Micah must have managed to go through the stronghold without setting off any of the traps. Nonetheless, I managed to destroy his bed in particular, meaning that his spawn point has been reset," Jerry assured me.

"We should go inside and see if we can find him," I said to him.

"Come on! But make sure you stay behind me and follow my every step. Keep your eyes peeled; I planted several traps that lead to a whole stack of TNT down in the basement."

"I'll be sure to be careful," I assured Jerry.

We ran into the stronghold and started looking for clues. After we swept all the rooms we found a tunnel in the library. Apparently, Micah was in such a rush to escape that he didn't even bother to seal the door behind him and cover his tracks, which was lucky for us. On the other hand he could have just let the door open for us to find so that we could just as easily walk right into a trap. Luckily, it wasn't the case, as we managed to find Micah at the end of the tunnel, inside a small room, while he was busy trying to build a portal to the Nether, through which he could escape. The portal was almost ready for using - the outer ring of obsidian block was complete. All that he had to do was light up a fire within it using his flint and steel.

Micah was just about to do that very thing when Jerry and I walked into the room.

"Don't move, Micah!" I shouted.

"Even if you manage to go through the portal we will still find you, you know. We will just follow you through the portal and into the Nether, Micah," said Jerry.

"You have got nowhere to go, Micah. End of the line, buddy!"

But instead of surrendering, Micah just laughed.

"Do you guys have any idea who you're going up against? Like, any idea whatsoever? You are not just going up against me, here. You are going up against Herobrine. Do you think he will just let you foil our plans?"

"And what exactly are your plans, might we ask" said Jerry.

"I'll scratch his back and he'll scratch mine, that's what the plan is. We all know Herobrine. We've all heard the legend, the myth. He appears from time to time, he stalks unsuspecting players and he torments them. He has these creepy, scary temples that seem to pop out where you least expect him to be. Nobody knows who he is or what he wants. I don't even know who he is, but I don't care. I've made a deal with him, you see. I'll help him gather all he needs to build his doomsday device that will help him appear wherever he wants and whenever he wants, all over every world. That's right! He won't just appear randomly like a some bug or some glitch, he will appear everywhere and anywhere he pleases to bring annihilation to all who oppose him!"

"Wow. But won't that mean that he will bring destruction and annihilation to this world, too?" I asked Micah.

"No! You see, that is the whole beauty of this deal that he and I have made. I help him rule over Minecraft and do whatever he pleases to do and in return, he grants me protection and absolute power over this world!"

"Why can't you just have fun in Minecraft like the rest of us?" I asked him.

"Fun? Fun! I tried to have fun back when I first spawned here. I tried to be creative and have a good time. Do you know what happened? Griefers! All sorts of players came here griefing and ignoring the rules! Do you think I never wanted to make friends and have a good time? Do you? My friends and I built a nice village, we built farms and animal shelters and we even built a nice rollercoaster. But those griefers came and spoiled the fun for all of us. They came and they destroyed everything until players no longer wanted to come here. This place was full of players. They used to come here and have fun. Now this place is a barren wasteland. But not anymore! Griefers will forever be banished from here thanks to Herobrine! And thanks to me!"

"You are kind of crazy, Micah," I told him, "no offense, but do you really think that Herobrine will just let you rule over this world?"

"Yeah, Micah. Are you sure that he is really going to keep his end of the bargain? What makes you so sure that he will go through with his promise? Herobrine is evil and you know it! He won't keep his word and we will all pay the price of it, including you, Micah!" said Jerry.

"Liars! You are both liars and griefers! You've come here to destroy what I've accomplished! Look at what you have done to my village! We took you in, we offered you a home, Jerry!"

"You've destroyed far more villagers, Micah! You've destroyed countless more, including my friends. Those guys only wanted to have a good time building things in Minecraft." I told him. "It is you who is the griefer!"

Micah didn't like hearing me call him a griefer. He suddenly lost his talkative mood. He opened up his inventory and took out some poison bottles and started throwing them at us at an alarmingly fast pace.

We barely managed to escape the black rain of poison that came towards us.

When Micah ran out of poison to throw at us he equipped his enchanted diamond sword and started hacking and slashing at us with incredible speed. Jerry turned around and ran down the tunnel, leaving me alone to face Micah.

I did a pretty decent job fighting Micah, but he was simply too powerful for me, He had powerful enchantments on all of his items, making him fast, difficult to hit and granting more power to his attacks. I was feeling pretty much helpless at that point.

But then I heard Jerry calling me from the tunnel.

"Come on, Mike! He will surely kill us both! Run, he can't catch us if we run!"

I instantly turned around and bolted through the narrow tunnel towards the sound of Jerry's voice. Jerry kept telling me to run faster and kept taunting Micah. When I finally got out of the tunnel I jumped into the room and saw that Jerry had placed TNT blocks all around the tunnel's exit. Not only did I see that but I also saw Micah, coming towards us rapidly with his enchanted sword in his hand, ready to deliver what he thought would be the final blows. And so when Micah approached the end of the tunnel, Jerry activated the TNT blocks and once Micah reached the exit the TNT exploded. The explosion was so big that it managed to hurt both Jerry and me, but when we looked to see if the explosion had destroyed Micah, we saw him running back through the tunnel and towards the portal to the Nether. By the time that Jerry and I caught up to him, he had already managed to light the fire inside the portal and activate it and was halfway teleported beyond.

It seemed that all of the enchantments that Micah had put on his diamond set of armor and all of the potions that he must have consumed had kept him safe from the blast. Nevertheless, we both knew that we surely must have sustained a lot of damage, making him easier to defeat the moment we caught him.

After Micah teleported himself through to the Nether, Jerry and I followed him swiftly. When both of us reached the Nether we saw Micah running not far in front of us.

As I looked ahead of where Micah was running I could see that he was heading to what looked like a fortress. I could see several other Nether portals that were opened in the vicinity of the fortress. It seemed that this was one of his favorite hiding spots. The fortress had had the form of a very solid tower, being twice as tall as his stronghold, but it was built on a much smaller surface. Around the tower was quite a wide lava moat, with a bridge that led to the main entrance. It appeared that the gate was wide open.

Micah made his way up to the entrance and rapidly crossed the moat, going into the tower. Jerry and I weren't that far behind him. Once we entered the fortress we saw Micah running up the stairs, in an effort to reach the top of the tower.

While we ran up the stairs, Jerry equipped his bow and started firing arrow after arrow, trying to hit Micah. But Micah, being as fast as he was, proved to be a difficult target. For every five arrows that Jerry fired from his bow, only one would actually hit Micah. But the arrows that hit managed to slow him down. And by the time that he had reached to top of the tower, Jerry and I had managed to get within a few feet of him. Once Micah reached the top of the tower he bolted towards yet another Nether portal. He approached the portal and when he started to teleport, Jerry launched his last arrow. The arrow hit its mark. Micah was hit right in the middle of his diamond breastplate. The impact knocked him back through veil of purple energy and prevented him from being teleported to his destination in the Overworld. I then jumped through the portal and landed right in front of Micah. I then started to hit him with my diamond sword. The blows knocked him back to the edge of the platform. On one side, there was Jerry and me, swords in hands, waiting for him, on the other side there was a massive fall at the end of which there was a fiery lake of molten hot lava. Micah had nowhere to go.

Jerry slowly walked closer and said:

"End of the line, Micah. If you respawn you will lose your gear and be far away, too far to be of any help to Herobrine."

"Jerry is right!" I said. "You'll be of no use to Herobrine. But don't worry, we will still get him!"

Micah wasn't showing any sign of giving up.

"You guys don't understand! You cannot defeat Herobrine! He is unstoppable! He will come back. He always does. And when he does, he will be angry."

"You can still do it, Micah! You can still make up for your wrong doings! There is still a way. You can join us. The three of us stand a better chance of destroying Herobrine. We can do this together!" I said, still trying to convince him to surrender, after all that he had done.

"Come on, Micah! You know he is evil. You know what he does to players!" said Mike.

Micah turned around, facing the lava.

"What about what players do to players?"

He then turned around and started throwing poison potions at Jerry, who was the closest to him. Almost all of the potions managed to hit Jerry, inflicting a great amount of damage to him. All it took was one single swing from Micah's enchanted diamond sword and my best friend Jerry turned into a cloud of smoke and disappeared. I stood there and watched as all of his belongings fell down on the floor and little flashing orbs hovered near the place where he stood.

Micah's attention then turned to me. He swung his sword at me, but I managed to stay clear of its blade. I then responded with swings of my own. All of my hits landed on Micah's armor, knocking him further and further towards the edge, until finally, with one last blow, I sent him falling to his doom. He fell all the way down and plunged into the lava moat that surrounded his own fortress. His fancy armor and all of his potions and enchantments didn't manage to save him from the lava.

I stood there for a while. I thought about my friend Jerry and I wondered where it was that he respawned. Did he respawn back at the village? Did he respawn on the mountaintop where we first had spawned into this world?

All I knew was that I didn't have much time to spend looking for him. I had to find Herobrine and put an end to all of this destruction.

I walked back in forth on the top of that tower thinking of all the places where I could find Herobrine. I was circling the portal when the answered appeared. Well, actually to put it more accurately, I was actually circling the answer, because the answer was the portal itself. Where did Micah so desperately try to go, if not back to Herobrine? He was cornered and wounded; his team of acolytes had been defeated. It was fairly obvious that the one place that he was so desperately trying to reach was in fact, the place that his master, Herobrine was.

Without wasting any more time, I walked through the portal.

When I reached the Overworld I saw that I was transported into a forest. I turned around and I saw the mountain, not far away in the distance. But what I saw next was pretty scary. Not only did I saw that the purple beam of light that was coming from the temple where we found Micah and his goons was still firing up into the sky, but I also saw that there was yet another identical temple that was built on the other side of the mountain, firing an identical beam of purple energy up into the sky. And when I looked up I saw that the sky had turned red in the two places where the energy hit it and that the moon was slowly fading away.

I opened up my inventory and I saw that even after collecting some of the things that Jerry dropped after being destroyed by Micah, I was still unprepared to deal with someone as powerful as Herobrine. But I had no choice, really. Something had to be done. It was either that I stop Herobrine now, or he would carry out his plan and become some sort of overlord not just over this world, but also over all of Minecraft.

With that in mind I started running towards the mountain.

I managed to quickly find the road that led to the mountain. But it was there that I saw yet another scary sight. The whole road was full of hundreds upon hundreds of mobs: zombies, endermen and spiders and creepers and even witches. All of them were marching towards the mountain. Thankfully, all of them were ignoring me. All of them were blindly marching towards the mountain, as to form a giant parade that would welcome Herobrine as their new king.

When I finally got close to the mountain I saw it: the two beams of purple light expanded and formed a huge portal. And out of the portal came a huge, apocalyptic contraption that slowly made its way into the Overworld. Light beamed across the night sky, crisscrossing all over the place, hitting the ground and the trees and at the top of the portal the sky turned dark red, looking a lot like the Nether. The water in the rivers that once flowed from the foot of the mountain turned into lava and a powerful shockwave disintegrated all the nearby trees. And probably the scariest thing that happened was that from the portal came a huge black dragon.

The dragon screamed so loud that you could feel the earth tremble. He then spread his dark wings and glided across the sky, firing a giant beam of purple energy into the portal.

The portal seemed to draw power from the dragon's blast of energy. The evil contraption that slowly crept out of it seemed to increase its pace.

I watched all of these things unfold from within the whole parade of monsters that was marching towards the portal.

It was then that I realized why the monsters had come and why Herobrine needed all of those precious resources. Next to where the giant portal was a huge black hole that gaped its void from the ground. All the monsters were marching towards the black hole and went down it. As the black hole swallowed all the zombies, skeletons, enderman, spiders and witches, the portal grew stronger and Herobrine's evil contraption came into the Overworld much faster.

The resources were also used as fuel for the portal, all of them being melted into blocks, being stored into mine carts and thrown down the black hole.

Witnessing all of this was Herobrine himself, patiently overseeing everything and patiently waiting for it to be over.

When he finally reached the portal, I walked out of the giant herd of monsters and walked up to Herobrine. His back was turned, as he was facing his evil contraption that was getting bigger and bigger. I was getting no more than ten feet of him, sneaking my way closer, hoping for a surprise attack, when he suddenly turned around. I completely froze.

I stood like that for about ten seconds, not knowing what to do next. Herobrine didn't move an inch. He just stood there looking at me with his big white eyes. He didn't say anything either. He just stood there.

It was then that I finally decided to go all out and attack him. I swung my sword at him, trying to aim for his head, but he moved out of the way at the last moment. I swung again. I missed again. I swung yet again. And I missed again.

At that moment he took out a simple iron sword and started swinging at me. One single blow was enough to knock me back five feet and take away a large amount out of my health bar. I turned around and ran, avoiding his impending attack.

There was something weird about him. I mean, I know he is Herobrine; he is the definition of the word "weird". But still, there was something very unsettling about him. First off, he wasn't that fast. Micah would have run circles around him. And he fought me using what looked like a simple iron sword and no armor.

Nevertheless, he was deadly. Another direct hit from that sword of his and I would have been toast.

I ran from him, toward one of the temples. But I soon found out that that was a big mistake. I only took my eyes off him for a second, when I focused on the temple ahead of me and that was all it took for him to use some of his "special" abilities and pop up right in front of me. I stopped and braced myself for the incoming blow.

But the blow never came, as Herobrine focused his attention on something else. His evil contraption had made its way out of the portal and into the Overworld entirely.

The apocalyptic machine looked horrifying. It looked like a huge tower that was made out of obsidian, nether bricks, diamond blocks and gold blocks. On its sides it had pistons that stuck out and went back and when they stuck out, lava would come pouring out. The whole thing looked like a giant blade. The doomsday device had rows of glow stone that lid up in a strange sequence. The sinister tower also had what looked like a command room, somewhere near the top. And it also looked like Herobrine was in a hurry to reach it.

Herobrine started running towards his tower of doom. I followed him closely while I downed the two health potions that I had gotten from Jerry.

"I sure could have used Jerry's help right about now," I thought to myself.

I got stayed on Herobrine's tail while he made his way through the large group of monsters that kept coming.

Somehow, even after all of the monsters saw me attack Herobrine, they still didn't attack me. They still kept running towards the black hole and they kept throwing themselves inside it when they reached it.

It was then that I thought of a way in which I could slow down the whole thing. As I ran through the masses of monsters I kept hitting the creepers that I passed while chasing down Herobrine. Eventually, one of them exploded, causing a chain reaction with the other creepers that were in his immediate vicinity. The explosions continued until a creeper exploded right next to Herobrine. The explosion knocked Herobrine back just enough so that I could get closer to him.

Unfortunately, the explosion didn't hurt him at all it seemed. He kept running. At one point he stopped and looked up towards the top of his tower. I did the same and saw that something up there was attracting the dragon's attention. The massive winged lizard kept circling the top of the tower.

The glow stones on the sides of the tower started powering up in sequence, starting from the bottom and going all the way up to the command room and the very sharp tip.

Herobrine started climbing the stairs that went all the way up to the command room. Naturally I followed him. As we made our way further up to the command room I started seeing withers, ghasts, magma cubes and blazes come out in whole legions out of the portal. The shockwave that spread from within the portal started expanding and disintegrating even more trees. As I got higher up the tower I could see further into the distance as far as the village and all the trees and the grass were gone.

I had to reach Herobrine and find a way to stop all of this before it was too late.

We had almost reached the command room, when out of nowhere the dragon started firing his beam of energy straight at the tower. Herobrine stopped for a moment and looked at where the dragon was firing. He then looked at the dragon and somehow the ugly creature understood that he had to stop. Herobrine then looked at me. The dragon let out a powerful scream and then started flying right at me, firing his energy beam straight at me. I managed to dodge it by a hair and kept running up the stairs, hoping that I would catch up to Herobrine before he managed to activate whatever he had in order to finish his sinister grand plan. But between dodging the incoming attacks that the ghastly dragon was sending my way and managing not to lose my sight of Herobrine I saw an interesting thing. As Herobrine ran up the stairs, from time to time there were small explosions that kept knocking him down and leaving small dents into the side of his sinister tower.

Of course, I didn't have much time to wonder about what it was that caused those explosions, because all I wanted to do was stop Herobrine.

When we finally reached the end of the stairs and got into the control room, Herobrine started frantically pulling levers left and right.

The control room was a rather big room, with wide windows. In the center of the room there was a sort of pillar that was made out of diamonds. The pillar had a small square right in the middle of it. The square was empty, apart from a small orb of energy that floated right in the middle of it. On the walls of the room there were a series of seven levers.

By the time that I reached Herobrine, he had already managed to pull down two of the levers.

Outside, the black hole grew bigger and bigger with each series of monsters that it swallowed. And as the black hole grew bigger, the portal grew stronger. And finally, as the portal grew stronger, the doomsday tower's lights flashed brighter and brighter.

This was to be the final part of Herobrine's plan. When the doomsday device was fully charged he would fire it up and he would become the overlord.

Herobrine went for the third lever, when I leapt and hit him with my sword. The blow sent him back about two feet. He turned and gave me a blank stare. But when he was about to return the favor and try and hit me with his own sword, an explosion went off behind him and threw away from the command console. Herobrine flew out of the room through the wide doorway. But unfortunately the blast didn't manage to destroy the console. I then started smashing the nearest lever with my sword. But I didn't manage to destroy it, because Herobrine was already backing inside the room. He hit me with his iron sword and sent me flying through the room and hitting the wall the pillar that was in the middle of the room. When I crossed the room to try and attack Herobrine once again, I saw a small orb fly past my head. The small orb smashed against the console and vanished. And in the place where the orb had vanished, appeared a player. He was wearing a full set of enchanted diamond armor and he wielded an enchanted diamond sword.

"Well don't just stand there! Come help me defeat Herobrine," he said.

And at that moment I realized who it was. It was Micah. He had managed to find his way up here after he respawned and decided that he was going to help me stop Herobrine.

Then both of us started attacking Herobrine with our swords from both sides. We landed almost every blow, but Herobrine didn't seem to take much damage. He flashed red from time to time, maybe once every ten hits, but other than that he wasn't taking damage at all. After a short time, he decided that this whole charade was going on for too long. And so, he turned around swiftly and with his blade, he sent me flying across the room once more. He then focused his whole attention on Micah. Micah took a lot of punishment as Herobrine kept pressing onward with his attack. Micah then turned around and equipped another one of his ender pearls and threw it next to where I was standing. He teleported himself right next to me and said:

"Listen, kid. Take all of this dynamite, carve yourself a hole next to the pillar and jump down. Place as much dynamite you can, as fast as you can and blow it up. I'd advise you to get as far away possible from the blast as you can. Oh, and here! Take this," he said as he dropped a diamond pickaxe to the floor. "Good luck! And tell your friend that I'm sorry!"

And with that he turned around and charged straight at Herobrine, trying to prevent him from pulling the last two levers.

I quickly equipped the diamond pickaxe that Micah gave me and started digging a hole right next to the pillar. Soon enough I had dug my way down into a small room that was directly underneath the command room. The room was filled with glowing orbs that started flying out of the room and through the hole I had just made. But as those flew away, others took their place, coming in from what looked like vents that were on the walls.

I then filled the room up with TNT blocks. Once the room was full of dynamite I climbed out of it and sealed it with other blocks of dynamite placed e line of TNT blocks that went next to the console. Micah was still battling Herobrine. The two of them were on the far side of the room. Micah was facing me, and saw what I was doing.

"Detonate them, man! Do it!" He yelled.

I took out my flint and steel and used it to activate five of the TNT blocks. The blocks fizzled. And as I turned around and started running down the stairs I could hear Micah saying.

"So much for your doomsday device, Herobrine. You griefer!"

And then the dynamite exploded.

Somehow the blast from the TNT managed to detonate some of the mechanism or maybe it was the fuel, from within Herobrine's tower. Whatever it was, the resulting explosion was huge. At first, the top of the tower exploded and then that triggered a chain of explosions going down, towards the base of the tower. Of course, the explosions went down faster than I could ever climb down those stairs. One of the explosions sent me flying into the air.

But as I was falling I could see the shock waves spreading and all of the nasty things that came out of the portal came rushing back. By the time I had hit the ground, everything was back to normal and just before everything went dark, I could see that the beauty was restored to the world and that all of those nasty, dark things, along with Herobrine were nowhere to be seen.

Epilogue

When I respawned I was by a small pond. I walked around and I looked at every beautiful color. The nice yellow flowers, the red mushrooms, the green grass and the trees. I even saw a bunny, I think.

I knew that I had lost all of my items and that I needed to get others fast. Herobrine and his ilk may have been banished from here, but that didn't mean that the other Overworldly mobs wouldn't be coming out at night. I knew all that, but I couldn't help but wander through the forest just for a couple minutes more.

I felt that I had accomplished so much.

I felt that it was the greatest adventure that I ever had. Who would have thought that I, Mike the Noob, would live such a great adventure and be the one that saved Minecraft from Herobrine's reign.

I walked around for a couple more minutes. After that I chopped down a tree, crafted myself an axe, a pickaxe and a shovel. After that I built myself a small cabin. And when the night came I was indoors, enjoying a nice bowl of mushroom soup.

Days passed and I built myself quite an impressive house and a farm to go with it. I even managed to find some horses. It was nice to get some peace and quiet.

But soon enough, I started yearning for another great adventure. I guess I wanted to feel the thrill of a treasure hunt, or the feeling that you get when you're out there, discovering new places, crafting all sorts of stuff, traveling through to the Nether.

One day, I saw two players approaching my farm. I got on my horse and rode off to meet them.

And it was that day that I met up with Jerry and Micah. They came with news of another adventure…

But that's a story for another time.

The End